Anna, Banana,

and the
Puppy
Parade

Anna, Banana,

and the
Puppy
Parade

Anica Mrose Rissi

ILLUSTRATED BY Meg Park

SIMON & SCHUSTER
BOOKS FOR YOUNG READERS
New York   London   Toronto   Sydney   New Delhi

SIMON & SCHUSTER BOOKS FOR YOUNG READERS
An imprint of Simon & Schuster Children's Publishing Division
1230 Avenue of the Americas, New York, New York 10020

SIMON & SCHUSTER BOOKS FOR YOUNG READERS is a trademark of Simon & Schuster, Inc.
For information about special discounts for bulk purchases, please contact Simon & Schuster Special Sales at 1-866-506-1949 or business@simonandschuster.com.
The Simon & Schuster Speakers Bureau can bring authors to your live event. For more information or to book an event, contact the Simon & Schuster Speakers Bureau at 1-866-248-3049 or visit our website at www.simonspeakers.com.
Book design by Laurent Linn
The text for this book is set in Minister Std.
The illustrations for this book are rendered digitally.
Manufactured in the United States of America
1215 FFG
2 4 6 8 10 9 7 5 3 1
Library of Congress Cataloging-in-Publication Data
Rissi, Anica Mrose.
Anna, Banana, and the puppy parade / Anica Mrose Rissi ; illustrated by Meg Park.—
First edition.
pages cm
Summary: Sadie, Isabel, and Anna decide to enter Banana into a puppy parade to raise money for the local animal shelter, but when Sadie and Isabel get really involved, helping to bathe, brush, and get Banana ready for the big day, Anna starts to feel possessive about her dog.
ISBN 978-1-4814-1614-6 (hardcover)
ISBN 978-1-4814-1616-0 (eBook)
[1. Friendship—Fiction. 2. Dogs—Fiction.] I. Park, Meg, illustrator. II. Title.
PZ7.R5265Anu 2016
[Fic]—dc23
2015003163

For my parents
(and Schnippy, Chance, and Hund)
—A.M.R.

Anna, Banana,

and the
Puppy
Parade

Chapter One
Would You Rather

"Okay, I've got one," my best friend Sadie said. "Would you rather have your own magic unicorn, but you have to keep it a secret, or have a regular horse that isn't magic but everyone can know about it?"

"The unicorn," my other best friend, Isabel, said immediately. "Who wouldn't choose the unicorn?"

Sadie swallowed a mouthful of her peanut butter and banana sandwich. "I wouldn't. I'd choose the horse so I could ride him to school and show him off to people and stuff. Horses aren't magic but they're still beautiful." She looked at me. "What about you, Anna?"

I chewed a slice of apple while I thought. This was a hard one. Sadie was really good at this game. "I'm not sure," I said. "I'd love to have a unicorn, but I can't keep secrets from Banana." Banana always seems to know what I'm thinking. That's part of what makes her the best dog ever.

Sadie grinned. "Telling Banana wouldn't count."

"Okay, but I'd also want to tell you guys," I said. "So I choose the horse." I pictured the three of us riding through a field on a chestnut mare. We'd braid her mane and brush her coat until it shined, and I'd always keep sugar cubes in my pockets for her. The best part of having a horse would be sharing her with my friends.

"My turn," Isabel said. "Would you rather be a famous actor or a famous singer?"

"Actress!" Sadie said.

"Singer," I said.

"Me too. We can sing duets," Isabel said to me.

"Hey, then I want to be a singer too!" Sadie said. "No, wait. I'll still be a famous actress and you guys can sing the sound tracks for all my movies."

"Deal," Isabel said.

It was my turn to ask a question next. I looked around the lunchroom for inspiration. "Hmm. Would you rather look like a troll but smell like roses, or be super pretty but always smell like the school cafeteria on hot-dog day?"

"Ew!" Sadie said. We all burst into giggles.

Banana loves hot dogs, which is funny because she's also shaped like one, all long and skinny in the middle. The hot dogs we eat at home are tasty, but today's hot lunch smelled like ketchup and skunk stew.

At least the ketchup came in packets instead of squeeze bottles, so we didn't have to listen to ketchup farts while we ate. My brother gets those bottles to make the grossest sounds possible. He's disgustingly good at it.

"I'd be a nice-smelling troll, definitely," Isabel said when she'd caught her breath.

Sadie scrunched up her nose and shook her head. Her curls bounced. "I can't answer this one," she said.

"We'd still love you if you smelled like school lunch," I promised her.

"We'd just love you from a little farther away," Isabel teased.

Sadie stuck out her tongue. She folded up her sandwich wrapper and wiped her lips with a paper napkin. As usual, Sadie's side of the table was much neater than Isabel's and mine. Though most of the mess on our side was Isabel's.

Isabel stuffed her own trash into her lunchbox. "Oh! I almost forgot," she said, pulling out a piece of paper. "I brought you a surprise." She smoothed out the wrinkles and thrust the paper at me. "Ta-da!"

Chapter Two

Paws on Parade

I took the light blue paper from Isabel's hand and saw the word "puppy" on it, upside down, in all capital letters. Before I could even turn the page right-side up, Sadie was leaning across the table to look. "What is it?" she asked.

I read it out loud. "'Calling all pups for the Puppy Parade! Paws, prizes, treats, tail-wagging, music, and more.'"

Isabel shimmied in her seat. "It's perfect, right? They were handing them out at the grocery store," she said.

"Let me see," Sadie said. She pulled the paper out of my hands.

"Hey! I wasn't finished," I told her.

"Sorry." She handed it back. Sadie can be pretty bossy sometimes, even with her friends, but I'm learning to stand up for myself when I need to.

I kept reading. "'Bring your family and your fabulous furry friend for a day of fun at the Happy Homes Animal Shelter's first annual dog show. Parade starts at the east entrance of Piddleton Park at 10 o'clock sharp. Refreshments provided by Rosie's Bakery and Yip Yap Yums.'" I looked up at my friends. "That's the shelter where we got Banana. This sounds like so much fun!"

Sadie reached for the flier again and this time I let her take it.

"You have to enter Banana," Isabel said. "She'll win for sure."

Sadie was nodding. "Banana is definitely Best in Show," she said. Best in Show was the top prize in the dog show Sadie and I watched on TV last year, back before we met Isabel. We'd seen so many cute dogs, all fancily groomed and well behaved—but no dog was as special as Banana, I thought. I was glad to hear my friends agreed.

I imagined Banana in a sparkly gold collar, marching past the judges with her ears perked and

her tail in the air. I pictured myself in a matching gold headband, holding Banana's leash and smiling proudly as the crowd gasped at her cuteness. Banana would be a star. And that would make me a star too.

"'Saturday the twelfth,'" Sadie read. "That's this weekend. We only have two days to get ready!"

We? I hadn't pictured Sadie and Isabel being in the parade—I'd assumed it would just be Banana and me. But of course Sadie and Isabel would walk with us. It would be even more fun with my best friends by my side. I'd still be the one holding the leash, though, so everyone would know that Banana is my dog.

"Good thing we're having a sleepover at your house tomorrow," Sadie said, pushing the flier back across the table. "There's so much to do.

We need to start planning right away."

"We do?" I said. I was excited about the parade and the sleepover too, but I wasn't sure what kind of planning Sadie had in mind.

"Yes!" Sadie jumped up as the bell rang. The cafeteria filled with the clanging and banging of kids all around us rushing to bus their trays. "I'll make a to-do list and write down ideas."

"And I'll help!" Isabel said as she and Sadie started for the door.

I grabbed my lunch bag and hurried after them, feeling weirdly left out. Banana was *my* dog. Why was Sadie in charge of the parade plans? "Then what am I supposed to do?" I asked when I'd caught up.

"You'll add ideas too," Sadie said. "We're all in this together, right?"

"Right!" Isabel cheered, and I realized I was being silly. They weren't trying to take over. They just wanted to be part of the fun.

"Right," I echoed. Sadie hooked her arms through Isabel's and mine, and we skipped down the hall back to class.

Chapter Three

Fraction Distraction

I tucked the dog show flier into my pocket and put my lunch bag in my cubby before sliding into my seat next to Isabel's. Our teacher, Ms. Burland, clapped twice to get everyone's attention and asked Justin and Keisha to hand out the worksheets we'd be using for math.

Justin walked up the first row of desks, making a big show of putting down each worksheet turned in the wrong direction. Sadie giggled as he plopped one onto her head instead of placing it on her desk. I rolled my eyes. Justin thinks he's so smart. I wished Sadie wouldn't encourage him.

When he got to Isabel, he delivered her work-sheet with a crash-landing sound, just quiet enough that Ms. Burland wouldn't hear it. Isabel said, "Thanks," and flipped it the right way around. I tried to think fast of something clever to say when Justin reached me, but he surprised me by putting the page down normally.

"Good," I mumbled. Justin smirked.

I tried to pay attention as Ms. Burland started the lesson on converting fractions into decimals and decimals into fractions, but my mind kept going back to Banana and the Puppy Parade. I wondered what other kinds of dogs would be there and what the prizes would be. Would Banana stand on a tall podium at the end, all high up above the crowd, and get a medal placed around her neck, like in the Olympics? Or would they put the medal around *my* neck and pin a first-place star to Banana's collar instead?

I wondered if there would be any TV cameras there. Maybe someone from Hollywood would see us and Banana would get discovered. She could be cast in a movie or star in her own show. Maybe she'd get her own channel! I'd watch Bananavision all day, if my parents would let me.

But I wouldn't actually have to watch Banana's show, since of course I'd be in it with her. We'd invite Sadie and Isabel to come be on it sometimes too, as special guest stars.

I picked up the supersparkly rainbow pencil I keep on my desk and imagined it was a glitter baton that I'd twirl and toss above Banana in the parade. I spun it around in my fingers and it flashed in the light before dropping to the floor with a *clang*. I quickly picked it back up. I'd have to practice my twirling before Banana and I got famous.

Ms. Burland's voice cut through my daydream. "I've never seen such a sleepy, distracted bunch of third graders," she said. "What did they feed you at lunch today? Was there a sleeping potion in the milk?"

Isabel shifted nervously in her seat. I could see from the kittens she'd been drawing in her notebook that she hadn't been paying attention either. At least I wasn't the only one. But still, I hated to disappoint Ms. Burland. I sat up straighter and tried to look focused.

"I know what you need," Ms. Burland said. Her voice was still stern but her eyes smiled. "Let's wake up those brains with a lightning-fast round of Beat the Calculator. Amanda and Sadie, you're up first."

Sadie squealed with delight as she jumped out of her seat, and Isabel and I shared a smile. Sadie loves math, and she loves competitions even more. Also, she's really good at this game—she's our reigning class champion. Her brain beats the calculator almost every time.

"Reign" was one of our words of the day last week. It means "to rule," like a queen or king does, but it can also mean "to be the best." Sadie reigns at math. Isabel reigns at drawing. Banana reigns at cuteness, which is why she'll reign at the dog show. I don't know what I reign at—maybe at remembering the word of the day. It's one of my favorite parts of school. That, plus art class and science projects, and the cool shoes Ms. Burland always wears.

Ms. Burland fetched the multiplication and division flashcards from her desk while Sadie and Amanda pushed two chairs together at the front of the room. "Hold on to those worksheets, because we're coming back to fractions and decimals when the game is over," Ms. Burland told us. Behind me, Justin groaned. "Now. Who gets the calculator?" Ms. Burland asked.

"I do!" Amanda said, reaching out to take it. Sadie nodded.

"Okay, you know the rules," our teacher said. "I'll hold up a flashcard and read you the problem. One person solves it with the calculator and the other person solves it in her head. Whoever gets the answer first calls it out. If a player gets two right answers in a row, and gets them fastest, she knocks out her opponent and stays to face the next challenger. Ready?"

"Ready!" Sadie and Amanda said together, and the game began.

Ms. Burland held up the first flashcard. "Three times three."

"Nine!" Sadie shouted.

"Correct," Ms. Burland said, and I beamed at my friend, practicing the winning smile I'd be wearing on Saturday when Banana got first place at the parade.

Chapter Four
Funny Bunny

"Banana!" I said as my brother, Chuck, and I stepped in the front door after school. Banana jumped and barked at our feet, excited as always to see us.

"Chill, jumping bean," Chuck said. He'd been crabby like that the whole walk home. I wondered if he'd gotten a bad grade on a test. Or maybe he was just hungry. He sidestepped Banana and headed straight for the fridge.

"Don't take it personally," I told Banana as I crouched down to pat her. She put her paws up on my knee and licked the tip of my nose.

I'm not really supposed to let Banana lick my face—Mom thinks I'll get dog germs or something—but Mom was still at work, so she'd never know. Besides, Mom lets *Chuck* kiss her face. That's way grosser.

I shrugged off my backpack and hung my coat on its hook. When I turned around, Banana was holding her favorite squeaky toy in her mouth. She tossed the yellow plastic rabbit into the air and caught it, then tossed it again and pounced on it. The rabbit squeaked as Banana shook it back and forth, growling and pretending to be ferocious. It was adorable.

"You'll be the cutest dog in the Puppy Parade," I said as I took the toy and sent it bouncing across the room. Banana ran after it.

"What puppy parade?" Chuck asked, setting

down the juice glass he'd emptied in one long chug.

I pulled the flier out of my pocket. "This one," I said. Chuck burped and took the paper. "Isabel and Sadie and I are going to enter her. It's this Saturday!"

"Hmph," Chuck said. "What if *I* want to enter her? She's my dog too, you know."

Banana dropped the toy at my feet as my jaw dropped in surprise. "But . . . but Isabel found the flier. And Sadie's making a list. We have plans!" I panicked. What if Chuck tried to ruin things? "Besides, I do most of her walks and feedings and stuff," I said. I didn't add, *so she's more my dog than yours*, but that's what I meant.

It seemed like everyone wanted to steal Banana away from me today.

Chuck snorted. "Just kidding," he said. "I won't rain on your parade."

My heartbeat slowed to its normal rate. I plucked the paper out of Chuck's hands. "Banana's going to be famous," I said. "Right, Banana?"

Banana wiggled in agreement, then sat at attention, hoping for a treat. I threw her one from the treats tin and she caught it in midair.

"That's my girl," I said firmly, just in case anyone needed to be reminded.

Chapter Five

Only a Dream

With the dog show and the sleepover both to look forward to, I was almost too excited to fall asleep that night. I lay awake, listening to Banana's soft doggy snores coming from her basket beside my bed. Mom had already come up to say good night ages ago, so I was well tucked in, but my body buzzed with so much energy, it was as if I'd eaten chocolate pasta with marshmallow meatballs and cotton-candy sauce for dinner instead of Dad's yummy lasagna.

When I finally fell asleep, I dreamed Banana and I were walking down the street with hundreds of other dogs, all up on their hind legs, twirling rainbow batons and playing clarinets and tubas in a marching-band parade. I spotted Isabel's braids and Sadie's ponytail way up at the front of the crowd, and Banana bounced ahead of me to join them. But I could only march as fast as the music was playing, and couldn't quite catch up to her and my friends.

It was a relief to wake up and find Banana right beside me, and sunshine streaming in through my window blinds. I climbed out of bed and peeked outside. It was a perfect day for a sleepover.

I shook off the strange dream and threw on a "Yay, Friday!" outfit of striped leggings and a smiley-face top. I grabbed a fat yellow ribbon that I'd saved off a present from Nana and Grumps, and was about to use it to tie back my hair when I got an even better idea. I bent down and tied it to Banana's collar instead.

"There," I said as I knotted the bow. "Now you're all fancy for the sleepover."

Banana wagged her whole backside. She looked like a wiggly little present. I bet when Isabel and Sadie saw her, they'd think the ribbon was so cute they'd insist she should wear it in the parade tomorrow, too. Maybe Mom could help us find more ribbons and we'd all wear them in our hair to match. Or maybe I'd cut this ribbon in half, and just Banana and I would share it.

"Banana, would you rather march at the front of the parade with Sadie and Isabel, or be stuck in the middle with me?" I asked. I didn't want to admit it, but I was still feeling a little funny about my dream.

Banana didn't even hesitate. She nudged my hand with her snout to show she'd choose me.

My heart flooded with relief, although of course Banana wouldn't ever really have to choose. Like Sadie had said, we were all in this together. And it was going to be super fun.

Chapter Six

A Spotty Plan

When Chuck and I got to school, Sadie and Isabel were already there. I spotted them across the playground, sitting on Isabel's favorite reading rock. I waved good-bye to Chuck and broke into a run.

My friends were so absorbed in whatever they were doing, they didn't even see me approach. "Hey," I said once I was standing right in front of them. I'd have climbed up onto the rock too, but there wasn't enough space for three.

Sadie and Isabel finally looked up from the notebook they were huddled over.

"Hi!" Isabel said, giving me a huge grin. She looked as delighted as Banana does when I scoop kibble into her bowl. "We brought all our sleepover stuff." Isabel pointed to the two back-packs and sleeping bags that were piled next to the rock.

"We've been writing down ideas for the dog show," Sadie said. "And I made us a schedule." She held up the notebook so I could see it too.

My stomach did a flip, as if it had been tossed in the air like Banana's bunny toy. It seemed wrong that Sadie and Isabel had been talking about the parade plans without me. Why couldn't they have waited until I got there?

But Sadie's eyes were shining proudly, and I knew she and Isabel had worked hard on this. I swallowed back the weird feeling and glanced at the page. "That's great," I said.

A funny look crossed Sadie's face. I must not have sounded convincing.

She dropped the notebook onto her lap. "It's just a start," she said. "We can add things. Or take stuff out. Or make a whole new plan."

I felt bad for how I'd reacted. "No, that's okay. It's a good schedule," I said, even though I hadn't really read it.

"Hey," Isabel said. She jumped off the rock. "Would you rather get the chicken pox or have to kiss a snake?"

Sadie and I laughed. Isabel is so random sometimes. But I was glad she'd changed the subject.

"I'd kiss the snake," I said. "I hate being itchy."

"Me too," Isabel said.

"Not me." Sadie shivered. "Snakes are all slithery. They give me the creeps."

"*Sssssssss,*" Isabel hissed, weaving her wrist back and forth like her arm was a snake. Its head twisted toward me and I leaned in to kiss it.

"*Mwah.* There! No chicken pox for me," I said.

"Now you're *sssssssssafe,*" Isabel agreed.

The bell rang and Sadie slid down off the rock. "Guess I'll be covered in chicken pox polka-dots for the parade," she said as she picked up her backpack. "Maybe I'll win Best Spots."

"Or Most Fowl," Isabel said. "Get it?"

Sadie giggled.

"Bawk, bawk!" I squawked, picking up the two sleeping bags. "Come on, sillies, let's get to class."

Chapter Seven
Bugging Out

The school day passed quickly. I got my spelling test back with a gold star at the top. We played kickball at recess with a bunch of other kids, and Isabel kicked a home run. I started a new book during silent reading time, about a funny dog who really wants to eat a hamburger. And the word of the day, "sprightly," was perfect for Banana. *Sprightly: full of energy*, it said on the whiteboard. I couldn't wait to get home and tell her about it.

When the final bell rang, Ms. Burland wished us all a happy weekend, and we set off for my house with Chuck. I carried Sadie's sleeping bag and Chuck took Isabel's. He's a surprisingly nice big brother sometimes.

"Would you rather carry a backpack filled with rocks everywhere you go, or have to do somersaults instead of walking?" Isabel asked as we marched along like we were in the Sleepover Parade.

"Backpack filled with rocks," Sadie said. "If you rolled everywhere, you'd get filthy."

"Why would I want to do either of those things?" Chuck said behind us.

Isabel stopped and turned around. "It's a game!" she said. "You have to choose one."

Sadie stopped too. "Those are the rules," she said.

"I'd do somersaults," I said. "That sounds kind

of fun." Besides, I was already sick of carrying the sleeping bag plus my backpack *not* filled with rocks, and we'd barely even gone a block. I'd happily tumble home now if it meant we'd get there faster. Dragging all this stuff around was making me cranky.

"I'd take the rocks," Chuck said. "No problem for a big stud like me." He puffed out his chest and flexed his arm muscles, like a wrestler on TV. Not that there was anything there to flex.

Sadie and Isabel laughed at the dumb joke, and Isabel showed off her muscles too. We'd

 never get home at this rate. But it seemed like nobody cared about that but me.

I shifted the sleeping bag to my other arm. "Can we please keep walking?" I said. It came out sounding more annoyed than I'd meant, but I was sick of standing around on the sidewalk while Chuck showed off for my friends. I wanted to get home to Banana so we could start the fun. My friends looked surprised, but at least they started moving again.

"I've got one," Chuck said, kicking my heels on purpose as we walked. "Would you rather eat a chocolate-covered ant or a chocolate-covered booger?"

"No!" I shrieked. Now I really was annoyed. Chuck was going to ruin our game with his gross-ness. And Sadie's giggles were only encouraging him.

"No, what?" Chuck said. "No chocolate? Fine. Would you rather eat an ant or a booger?"

I took a deep breath to keep myself calm. I knew Chuck was just trying to rile me up. That's what brothers do best. But still, it was hard not to scream.

"I've had a chocolate-covered ant," Isabel cut in.

"What?" I stared at her. "No way."

"Yup," Isabel said. "Last summer. My cousins dared me to eat it. It mostly tasted like chocolate, really."

"Whoa." Chuck looked impressed. Sadie wrinkled up her face and pretended to gag, but I think she was impressed too. "Maybe I'll ask Dad if he can make us chocolate-covered ants for dessert tonight," Chuck said.

"We're having personal pizzas and make-your-own sundaes," I informed him. "But you're welcome to put ants on yours."

"Pizza and sundaes, yum!" Isabel said. She twirled around in celebration, and soon Sadie and I were twirling too, spinning down the sidewalk until we were dizzy with glee.

"Weirdos," Chuck said, but we were having too much fun to care.

Chapter Eight
What's In a Name?

When we got home, Dad and Banana greeted us at the door. "Aw, look at her ribbon!" Sadie said. "Banana, you look adorable."

Banana yipped hello to my friends, and sniffed their overnight bags to see what they'd brought. Isabel giggled as Banana sniffed at her legs, too. "I bet she can smell Mewsic on me," Isabel said. Mewsic is Isabel's giant cat. Banana would probably love to play with her.

"Pull hard on that door to shut it tight behind you," Dad said to Chuck. "It's been acting a little tricky today." He loosened the tie he always wears while he's writing and asked, "Anybody want a snack?"

"Yeah!" I said. We followed him to the kitchen, with Banana right at our heels.

Dad made us popcorn while we sat at the table and told him about our day. When the popcorn was ready, he scooped out two servings for himself and Chuck to take, and left us alone with the rest. I reached into the big bowl and grabbed a handful. Banana gazed up at me with hopeful eyes. I tossed her a little piece of popcorn and she caught it on her tongue.

"So, what's first on the schedule?" I asked Sadie.

Sadie opened her notebook and turned to the list. "First we fill out the entry form," she said. "I got it off the parade website last night."

"I'll get a pen," I said, popping up to grab one from the jar on the counter. When I got back to my seat, Sadie handed me the printout.

"'Contestant's name,'" I read out loud. I uncapped the pen and, using my neatest letters, wrote *Banana*. "'Contestant's breed.' Wiener dog!" I said, moving my pen to the next line.

"Wait," Sadie said. "I think we should say 'dachshund.'"

"They're the same thing, right?" Isabel asked.

"Right," I said. "But I always call her a wiener dog. She likes it. Plus, it's easier to spell." Banana twitched her tail in agreement.

"But 'dachshund' sounds more sophisticated," Sadie said.

"True," Isabel said.

I hesitated. Banana is definitely more silly than sophisticated, and I liked the funny sound of "wiener dog," but Sadie and Isabel both looked so certain. "Dad!" I called over my shoulder. "How do you spell dachshund?"

"There's a dictionary in my office!" Dad answered from the living room.

My friends and I glanced at each other. Nobody wanted to go look it up.

Sadie sighed. "Okay, fine, just say wiener dog," she said. I wrote it in.

"'Owner,'" I read, and put down my full name. I went to the next line. "'Owner's addre—'"

"What about us?" Isabel interrupted.

I looked up. She and Sadie were both watching me expectantly. "What?" I said.

"Shouldn't our names go there too?" Isabel said.

I squinted, like that might help me see what she was thinking. "It says owner," I said. "And Banana is my dog."

"Of course she's your dog," Sadie said. "But we're entering her with you."

Isabel nodded vigorously. "Yeah, so our names should go on the form too," she said. "Because we're a team."

"I know we're a team. But it says *owner*," I repeated, trying not to sound upset. I didn't mind sharing Banana with my friends, but I didn't like feeling like they were trying to claim her as their own. That wasn't right.

Banana leaned against my legs to reassure me. But then a piece of popcorn fell from Isabel's fist, and Banana lunged under the table to grab it.

Sadie pressed her lips together. "Forget it," she said. "The form doesn't matter."

Isabel swallowed hard, like there was a big lump of popcorn stuck in her throat. "Yeah, it's fine," she said. But I could tell from her face that it wasn't.

I gripped the pen tighter. Maybe I should just write my friends' names in. Maybe it wasn't such a big deal. But for some reason, it felt like one.

"You know what?" Sadie said. "I think I'm done with popcorn. Let's take Banana to the spa."

Chapter Nine
Bubble Up

Isabel's eyes lit up. "The spa?" she said.

"Yup." Sadie gave a sharp nod. "Time to pretty her up. We'll wash her and brush her until she's the most beautiful dog you've ever seen."

I already thought Banana was the most beautiful dog I'd ever seen, but doing a dog spa did sound fun. Except . . . "Banana hates the water," I told them. "She won't even go wading at the beach. She barks like crazy when she sees the waves, and runs away if they touch her toes."

"Aw, that sounds adorable," Isabel said.

"Yeah, but everybody likes bubble baths,"

Sadie said. "We'll make it nice and fancy. She'll love it."

I peeked at Banana. She tipped her head to one side, curious. "Okay, let's try it," I said.

We raced upstairs to the bathroom. Banana went straight to the soft, fluffy bath mat in front of the tub. She turned in a circle twice, and lay down.

"What have you got for bubble bath?" Sadie asked.

I took out the bottle of Bumbleberry Bubbles that Nana and Grumps had sent. Sadie flipped open the cap and held it up to her nose.

"Hmm," she said. "Do you think your mom would let us use her lavender bath powder instead? That's even fancier." Sadie always loves admiring the pretty bottles and jars of nicely scented things Mom keeps in the other bathroom. Sometimes when we do our own sleepover spas, Mom lets us try her special hand cream or use her conditioner. Mom wouldn't be home until dinnertime, so I couldn't ask to use the powder, but I figured she probably wouldn't mind. Still, I felt uneasy about taking it without permission.

"We'll only use a little bit," Sadie said.

I looked at Isabel and Banana. Isabel shrugged, leaving it up to me. Banana thumped her tail.

"Okay, but just a little bit. And we have to put it back right away," I said.

Sadie grinned. "Great!" she said. I ran to get it. "And the lavender shampoo, too!" she called after me.

I paused for only a second before grabbing both. This was a special occasion. Mom would want Banana to be her best for the big parade.

When I got back to the other bathroom, Isabel was already running the water. Banana had moved off the bath mat, over to the far side of the room. She watched Isabel closely.

"It's okay, Banana," I said as I handed Sadie the two containers. "Baths aren't scary like the ocean." Banana flattened her ears. She wasn't convinced.

"And when you get out, you'll smell as

beautiful as you look!" Isabel told her. "Like a bouquet of lavender."

Sadie unscrewed the lid from the jar of bath powder and Banana lifted her nose, sniffing the air. My friends laughed. Sadie tipped the purple powder into the running water. A whole handful rushed out.

"Sadie!" I yelped. "That's too much!" Banana's ears shot straight up. The scent of lavender filled the room as a mound of bubbles piled up in the tub.

"Sorry," Sadie said. "I didn't think it would come out so fast."

I let my shoulders drop. They'd somehow made it all the way up to my ears. "That's okay," I said, trying to relax. Of course Sadie hadn't done it on purpose. "Let's just put the top back on before any more spills out."

Sadie tightened the lid while Isabel tested the water temperature and turned off the tap. Isabel scooped a pile of bubbles from the tub, held them to her lips, and blew. They shot toward me. I scooped up my own foamy handful and blew them back.

"Bubble fight!" Sadie cried, dipping both hands into the bubble mountain to get some soapy

ammunition. I shrieked and ducked as a glob of bubbles landed on my arm and another just missed Isabel's ear. Sadie giggled as I swatted a spray of them back at her. Banana yipped and jumped between us, nudging bubbles with her nose and batting them around with her fast-wagging tail.

"Bubbles away!" Isabel said as she stood and released a double helping of foam over Sadie's and my heads.

I was laughing so hard I almost didn't hear my dad call up the stairs, "Girls, are you making messes up there?"

"Nope, we're *cleaning* a mess—Banana!" I shouted back. I wiped the foamy bubbles off my cheek. "C'mere, Banana. Bath time!" I said. But Banana stopped her happy tail-wagging and backed away from the tub.

Chapter Ten

Pretty Is as Pretty Does

I called her again. "Come on, Banana! Don't be scared." I patted my lap, but Banana didn't budge. Sadie frowned.

I went over to the corner where Banana was hiding and knelt to stroke her ears. "I know you hate the water, but it won't be so bad. And think of how soft and pretty you'll be when we're done." I kissed her snout to reassure her. Banana still seemed uncertain, but she let me take off her collar and bow so they wouldn't get wet, and lift her in my arms.

I carried Banana over to the tub and lowered

her carefully into the water. Her whole body went stiff as she stood in the pile of bubbles with her ears pressed flat and her tail tucked between her legs. She did not look happy.

My heart lurched. I felt terrible making my dog do something she hated. But Sadie was right—Banana needed a bath to look as perfect as possible for the dog show. It wouldn't take long. And we'd definitely give her treats afterward.

"Good girl," I cooed in my most soothing voice as I drizzled warm water onto her back. Sadie and Isabel praised her too, and we all perched on the edge of the tub, patting her and getting her fur wet for the shampoo. Banana did not like the water, but she definitely liked the patting. Her ears perked up a bit, and I relaxed.

I squeezed a little dollop of the fancy shampoo

onto Banana's back. I rubbed some under her chin and soaped up her ears, being careful not to get any suds in her eyes, while Sadie and Isabel washed her back. Banana wriggled happily under the six-handed massage and the sweet-smelling lather.

"She likes it!" Isabel said. Banana nosed at the bubbles, getting a few on her snout. "A rub-a-dub-dub. A doggy in the tub!" Isabel sang.

When Banana was all soaped up, Isabel released the drain and Sadie grabbed the spray hose. "Time to rinse off!" she said. But when she turned on the water, Banana freaked. She squirmed out from under my grasp and lunged for the edge of the tub, trying to get away from the spray. But the bathtub was slippery and her paws couldn't get a grip, so she scrambled and splashed and slid around, getting water and bubbles everywhere.

"Banana, hold still!" I cried, trying to grab her. It was like trying to hold on to quicksand. Wiggly, slippery, soapy quicksand that was determined to jump out of the tub.

"Stay," Sadie commanded, turning off the spray, and Banana finally calmed down. She shook off, sending bubbles and water flying everywhere. It didn't matter. Everything in the bathroom was already soaked, including us.

Sadie handed me the spray hose. "Maybe you should do it," she said.

"I'm sorry, Banana, but we have to do this," I said as Isabel and Sadie each held on to her with both hands. "You can't go to the parade all covered in shampoo." I turned on the water and rinsed her off as quickly and gently as I could, while patting her with my free hand. Banana squeezed her eyes shut, wanting it to be over, but at least she stood still.

As the last of the bubbles swirled down the drain, I turned off the water and looked around us. There was dog hair everywhere. Bathwater and soap suds dripped down the walls, making puddles on the floor. Even the bath mat and the toilet paper roll were soaked. The bathroom was a disaster zone.

Banana shook off again, sending more droplets flying. "I'm going to get in so much trouble," I moaned.

"No, you're not," Sadie promised. "We can clean this up."

Isabel nodded. "We're in this together, remember?" she said.

Banana looked just as skeptical as I felt. I knew that if my parents saw this I'd probably never be allowed to have a sleepover again.

Sadie stood up and took charge. She pulled a stack of towels from the bathroom cabinet, handing one to me and two to Isabel. "You dry off Banana," she told me. "Isabel and I will take care of the rest."

I glanced at my sopping-wet dog. She stared back at me with huge eyes, wondering what torture was next. But when I unfolded the towel, she surprised me. Instead of backing away, Banana jumped out of the tub and lunged toward the towel, like an eager little bull charging a bull-fighter's cape. She burrowed into it, making playful growls. I rubbed her down as she spun around, turning it into a silly game.

When Banana was as dry as I could get her, I looked up and saw the bathroom gleaming. Sadie and Isabel had wiped down the walls and sopped up the mess with the extra towels. They'd replaced the ruined toilet paper roll with a new one from under the sink, and put the bath mat and towels straight into the washing machine. It was like the bath had never happened. "Wow," I said. My friends beamed.

The only thing still wet and messy was us. "Let's change into our pajamas now, and hang up our wet clothes to dry," Isabel said. "Then it will be a true pajama party."

We went back to my room and pulled on our PJ's. I heard the front door open and close, and ran to return Mom's stuff to the other bathroom before she could notice it was missing.

"Who wants pizza?" my dad called.

"We do!" I called back. Banana led the way downstairs to get it.

Chapter Eleven
Trick or Feet

After dinner and ice cream sundaes and helping clear and wash the dishes, we went back upstairs and sat on my rug and brushed Banana until she shined. She was extra soft and beautiful now, thanks to that bath. And she smelled nice, too. The judges were sure to be impressed.

Isabel got out a bottle of sparkly purple nail polish she'd borrowed from her oldest sister so we could paint Banana's toes, but Banana wasn't having it. She squirmed away from us and refused to sit still.

"Even if we get some on her toenails, it'll just

smudge off on the carpet before it dries," Sadie pointed out after our third failed attempt. "Let's paint each other's toes instead. We should look nice for the parade too."

"Yes! Good idea," I said, taking off my socks and tossing one to Banana. Banana caught it and shook it back and forth, wagging her tail. She may not have liked the spa, but she loves dirty socks.

"It's too bad, though," Isabel said as she wound a piece of Kleenex between her toes to keep them separated for the pedicure. "She'd really stand out if she had sparkly toes."

I wanted to jump in and defend Banana. She was already the best dog—she didn't need sparkly toes to stand out. But I swallowed back the words. I knew Isabel hadn't meant it to sound mean.

Sadie shook the bottle of nail polish and turned to me. "I'll do your toes, you do Isabel's, and Isabel will do mine," she said.

"Okay." I stretched out my legs toward Sadie. She unscrewed the cap, bent over my feet, and brushed a line of polish onto the first toe.

"So, what are Banana's talents?" Isabel asked.

I thought about it. "She's a really good listener," I said. "It's like she always knows how I'm feeling, even before I say it. She's fast, too—especially at grabbing food that drops. She's great at finding stinky things to roll in. And at being adorable and making me laugh."

"No, I meant

what tricks can she do," Isabel said. "Ways she can show off for the judges."

I looked at Banana. She turned to look behind herself, caught sight of her own tail, and spun in a circle, chasing it. "Well, she can chase her tail," I joked.

Isabel giggled, but Sadie frowned. "That's not really a trick," she said, moving on to the next toe.

Banana stopped spinning. Her tail drooped. I gave her a little head scratch to show it was okay.

"Can she sit? And shake?" Isabel asked.

"Of course she can sit," I said. "Banana, sit. Sit!"

Banana didn't sit. She ran to get her squeaky toy instead. "Oh yeah!" I said. "That's her best trick. She fetches the rabbit." I reached out to take the toy from her mouth, but Banana dodged my grasp. She didn't want to play fetch. She wanted to play keep-away instead.

"Hmm," Isabel said.

Embarrassment crept up my neck. "I mean, sometimes she plays fetch," I said. "But look, isn't she cute with the bunny in her mouth? She could carry it like that in the parade!"

Isabel tilted her head to one side, like Banana does when she's confused. "So her trick is that she likes her toy?" she asked.

My whole face felt hot. When Isabel put it that way, it suddenly didn't seem all that special.

"Never mind," I mumbled.

"There," Sadie said. "Don't your toes look great?"

Isabel leaned over to admire my feet. "Ooh,

pretty!" she said. I wiggled my sparkly toes and tried to smile, but it was hard to force it.

"Me next!" Sadie said. She scootched her feet toward Isabel and handed off the bottle of polish.

Banana nudged at my arm with her snout. "Banana, sit," I repeated. She plopped her butt down beside me. "Good girl," I said. "Isn't she good?" But Sadie and Isabel weren't paying any attention.

I petted Banana's silky ears. We didn't care what anyone else thought anyway.

At least, that's what I tried to tell myself.

Chapter Twelve
Too Much to Juggle

By the time our toes were all sparkling, it was getting pretty late. Banana stretched and yawned, sticking out her long pink tongue, while Sadie consulted her notebook. "We're a little behind schedule, but that's okay," Sadie said. "We can practice Banana's walk in the morning, before we brush her again."

"Let's brush her with olive oil to make her fur extra shiny," Isabel said. "My sister did that to her hair for the eighth-grade dance."

Banana swished her tail from side to side. She thought getting covered in olive oil sounded delicious. I wished that had been my idea.

Isabel blew on her toe polish to help it dry faster. "If there's a parade again next year, we should teach Banana how to juggle," she said. "But I guess there's no time tonight."

"Dogs don't juggle," I said.

Isabel changed positions so she could blow on her other foot. "I saw one do it in a cartoon once," she said. "He had three rubber balls that he hit with his nose and kept them all going while riding around on a unicycle."

"That would be amazing," Sadie said.

I crossed my arms. "Banana's not a cartoon!"

"Well, she wouldn't have to do the unicycle part," Isabel said.

"It's a dog show, not a circus," I said as calmly as I could. But I wanted to scream it.

My friends both looked at me. "Why are you so grumpy?" Sadie asked.

"I'm not grumpy!" I said. Banana's eyebrows scrunched together. I could tell she didn't believe me.

Isabel put her hand on my arm. "Don't worry," she said. "Banana's going to be great. Even without the juggling."

Sadie nodded firmly. "For sure," she said. She bugged out her eyes and sucked her lips into a silly fish face to cheer me up. I made the fish face back, pretending it had worked. I didn't want her and Isabel to think I was a spoilsport. But I hated feeling like they didn't think Banana was good enough.

"I know!" Sadie said. "We'll make her a costume." She ran to my closet and rummaged around. She pulled out the things I'd worn for last year's Halloween: wings, antennae, a tulle skirt, and a tiara. Sadie and I had gone as butterfly fairy princesses—that was before we'd met Isabel. We'd had the best costume in the whole second grade. But that didn't mean I wanted to put it on Banana. "Banana can wear the wings," Sadie said. "And maybe some of the other parts too."

"Yeah!" Isabel said.

"*No.*" I stomped my foot. Isabel's mouth fell open and Sadie dropped the costume. I looked at the floor to avoid their eyes. "The flier didn't say anything about costumes," I mumbled.

"So a costume will make Banana extra special," Sadie said.

"And it will be fun!" Isabel added.

"Banana's already special. She doesn't need wings or juggling or a unicycle," I said. I blinked hard, trying not to let out any tears. Doing the dog show together was supposed to be fun, but it didn't feel fun right now. It felt like Sadie and Isabel were ganging up on Banana and me, and trying to turn Banana into a completely different dog—a *better* dog. I wanted to shout, *Banana is the best dog there is!* but I knew they already thought I was being crazy.

Everyone was quiet. Finally, Sadie said, "You know what? I'm tired. Let's figure this out in the morning."

"Fine," I said.

"Fine," Isabel said.

We spread out our sleeping bags and brushed our teeth, and when Mom came in to say good night, Banana was already curled up in her basket beside me. "Don't stay up too late whispering," Mom said as she turned out the light. "Banana needs her beauty sleep to be ready for the parade."

"We won't," I promised.

And for the first time in the history of sleepovers, we didn't.

Chapter Thirteen
Bow-wow Meow

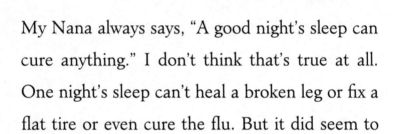

My Nana always says, "A good night's sleep can cure anything." I don't think that's true at all. One night's sleep can't heal a broken leg or fix a flat tire or even cure the flu. But it did seem to cure my bad mood.

I guess it's hard to wake up on the wrong side of the bed when you're not even in bed to start with. When I opened my eyes to the light of the morning—and to Banana pawing at my pillow and my friends sleeping beside me and the smell of Dad making us something delicious downstairs—I couldn't help but smile. All of my

grumpiness from the night before had floated away on a dream cloud. The almost-fight with my friends seemed almost silly now. It was hard to even remember why I'd been so upset.

I was glad I'd bitten my lip when I'd wanted to scream. That could have gotten really embarrassing.

I unzipped my sleeping bag and crawled out. Banana helped me nudge Sadie and Isabel awake. "It's parade day!" I said. Isabel blinked a few times, then sat straight up, her eyes bright with excitement. Sadie stretched and yawned, opening her mouth wide, just as Banana backed up and swished her tail right into it. Sadie yelped and turned over, smushing her face into her pillow. Isabel and I giggled, and Banana wagged even harder. She was glad too that the almost-fight seemed forgotten.

We rolled up our sleeping bags and got dressed for the parade, and followed Banana downstairs for breakfast. When we'd eaten our fill of waffles with butter and maple syrup, and Banana had gulped down her kibble, I clipped on Banana's leash. It was time to practice our parade walk.

We set out around the block with me in the middle, holding on to the leash, and Sadie and Isabel on either side of me. Banana darted ahead of us, sniffing one edge of the sidewalk and then the other.

"Can you do something to make her walk straight? It will look better if she doesn't zigzag at the parade," Sadie said. And just like that, the icky feelings from last night flooded back.

I tugged at the leash to get Banana's attention. "She's just looking for a good spot to pee," I told Sadie. "And sniffing out who else has been here. Dogs can tell a lot from their sense of smell. They're like nose detectives."

"Banana! The Private Investigator Pooch," Isabel said in a voice like a TV announcer.

Banana peed on a patch of grass, then walked straight in front of us like Sadie had wanted. Sadie hooked her arm through mine and Isabel did the same. I felt the tightness in my chest melt and loosen in the sunshine as we rounded the block in perfect step.

"You know what would be cool?" Isabel said, dropping my arm. "If she trotted like a show pony. You know how they lift their hooves up like this?" She demonstrated a pony prance.

Sadie joined in. "Giddyup, Banana!" she said.

Banana lifted one paw and wagged her tail apologetically. "I don't think she can do that," I said. Ponies have long legs that they can lift high, but Banana's only long in the middle. She has short legs and big paws. She's not built like a pony at all.

Sadie and Isabel didn't listen. They pranced in a circle around us. Isabel neighed.

"Stop it," I said. I didn't want Banana to feel bad. It wasn't her fault that her legs were short. Besides, she was adorable that way. But Sadie and Isabel were too busy prancing and neighing to hear me.

Sadie stopped beside me and held out her hand. "Maybe if I were holding the leash, she'd—"

"No!" I snapped. "I'm holding the leash! Banana is *my* dog."

Isabel froze midtrot. She and Sadie both stared at me. I pulled Banana closer.

"What's your problem, Anna?" Sadie said.

"My *problem* is that you keep trying to change everything about who Banana is!" I yelled.

"That's not true!" Sadie said. "We love Banana.

We're just trying to have fun. But all you want to do is be grumpy and shoot down our ideas."

"Yeah," Isabel said. "You keep acting like you don't even want us to be part of this. Like you don't want us on your team."

"Yes, I do!" I said. "But you keep trying to take over. Banana's my dog and I know her best, so I should get to have the final say."

Isabel put her hands on her hips. "If that's how you feel, maybe you should enter Banana all by yourself. Maybe I'll go home and get Mewsic, and Sadie and I will do the parade with her."

My mouth dropped open. "You can't enter a *cat* in a dog parade!"

"Oh yeah?" Isabel said. Her chin quivered as she turned away from me. "Hey, Sadie," she said. "Would you rather enter the parade with a cat or a big meanie?"

I snapped my jaw shut. It was the nastiest thing I'd ever heard Isabel say. I didn't even want to hear Sadie's answer. I ran into the house with Banana right beside me, before Sadie could reply.

We dashed up the stairs and into my room, and I slammed my door behind us. As soon as it was shut, my cheeks were covered in tears. Now that I'd started crying, it felt like I might never stop.

Banana looked at the door and looked at me. She whined softly.

"It's okay, Banana," I said, wiping my leaky eyes.

Banana did not look convinced.

Chapter Fourteen
Hide-and-Seek

Banana flattened her whole body against the carpet and put her nose up to the crack at the bottom of my door. She let out a huge sigh. With my sniffles and Banana's sighs, it was what my Nana would have called a Pity Parade. We were both feeling very sorry for ourselves.

I knew Banana missed Sadie and Isabel and wanted them to return. I did too. I was secretly hoping they had followed us inside and would come upstairs to apologize. As soon as they appeared, I'd apologize too. I didn't want us to be fighting.

I waited. No Isabel. No Sadie.

Fine. Banana and I were going to have plenty of fun in the parade without them. And they'd be sorry once Banana won Best in Show and got super famous.

I would probably accept their apologies and let them come visit us in Banana's new mansion-sized doghouse, with a sunroom for her and a waterslide for me, and golden bowls filled with dog treats and girl treats, plus lots of servants to bring us whatever else we wanted. But we wouldn't invite them to guest star on her TV show. And we wouldn't let Isabel bring along her dumb cat. There would be no cats allowed, for sure.

I blew my nose. There wasn't any more time for moping and crying. We needed to get ready to go to the parade.

I went to the bathroom to wash my face so no one would be able to tell I'd been crying. When my face was dry and my hair was combed, I went down to the kitchen to get the olive oil for Banana's fur. I wasn't really sure how much of it we were supposed to brush in, and I was a little bit worried it might just make a big mess, but Banana and I would figure it out. We didn't need Isabel or Sadie to help us. I tried to stop secretly wishing that they would.

"Okay, Banana," I said as I stepped into my room with the bottle. But Banana wasn't there.

"Banana!" I called. "Here, Banana!" I poked my head into the hallway, expecting to see her running toward me, ears flopping. But I didn't see her at all.

"Banana?" I tried again. "Banana, come!"

I peeked into the bathroom and my parents' room and Chuck's room, but Banana wasn't upstairs. I called her name as I went downstairs, thinking maybe she was in the kitchen or the living room, or even Dad's study. But Banana was nowhere to be found. I went back to the living room and checked under the couch. There were three dog toys underneath it, but no dog.

I stood in the kitchen and shook the container of dog treats, a sound that always, always brings Banana running. But this time, it didn't.

"Banana!" I shouted. "Where are you hiding?"

I moved back toward the front of the house, but as I reached the staircase, I froze. My heart sped up and my stomach dropped to my toes as I noticed something awful.

The front door was open.

It was open just wide enough for a small dog to slip through it and run outside.

Banana wasn't hiding. She was gone.

Chapter Fifteen
Doggone It

"Banana!" I screamed, racing out the door. My brain spun and my insides jerked like I was riding a Tilt-A-Whirl. I was dizzy with panic.

What if Banana had run into the street? What if she got lost or stolen, or was trapped someplace where she couldn't get out? Too many terrible things could happen. I had to find her, fast.

I rushed to the sidewalk and looked up the street in one direction, then the other. I couldn't see Banana, or any signs of which way she'd gone. So many minutes had passed before I'd noticed she was missing—by now she could be almost anywhere.

Why hadn't I been more careful? I should have remembered that the front door was acting tricky lately. I should have remembered to pull it shut tight behind me, but I'd been too upset about the fight with Isabel and Sadie. Now Banana was missing and it was all my fault. I should never have let this happen.

I ran around the side of the house, calling Banana's name. Maybe I'd be lucky and she'd just be in the backyard, chasing squirrels or digging up flowers. "Banana! Banana!" I shouted, stumbling across the uneven ground.

Banana didn't come running, but Sadie and Isabel did.

"What's wrong?" Sadie said, grabbing my arm. Her face was filled with worry.

I blurted the horrible truth. "Banana's gone! The front door was open and now I can't find her and I don't know which way she's run."

"Oh no!" Isabel cried.

But Sadie stood up straighter. "We'll help you find her," she said.

"Yes," Isabel said. "We know she didn't come this way because Sadie and I would have seen her. We've been out on the swing set this whole time."

"Right. So she must have gone that way, that way, or that way," Sadie said, pointing. "We'll split up and each take one direction."

Isabel squeezed my hand, hard. "We'll find her, Anna. She can't have gone very far."

I squeezed back, feeling terrified but grateful. Even after our big fight and how cranky I'd been, my friends were still there for me when I needed them most.

"Thank you," I said. There wasn't time to say anything more. We all set off in our separate directions, moving as quickly as we could. I called Banana's name and heard my friends calling her too. Hope mixed with the fear that was racing through my veins. Banana had to hear us. But why wasn't she coming when we called?

I tried not to think about the awful things that might have happened to her. We would find her. We had to. But I'd already walked so far and called so many times, and Banana was still gone.

I took a deep breath. "Banana!" I yelled once more.

Nothing.

Just when I thought I might collapse inside, I heard a small sound—a single bark.

"Isabel! Sadie!" I shouted. "This way!" I broke into a run.

Chapter Sixteen

A Nose for Trouble

I zoomed ahead at full speed, following the sound of the bark around the corner and into the backyard of a little yellow house near the end of my street. Behind the house was a big garden. And there, rolling in the compost heap, was a very filthy Banana.

"Banana!" I said as I ran to her. Banana stopped rolling in the disgusting pile of kitchen scraps and dirt, and wagged her tail, happy to see me. She picked up a rotten banana peel and trotted proudly over to show it to me. I threw my arms around her, crying with relief. She dropped the peel on the ground and licked away my tears.

She was muddy and stinky and covered in filth, but I didn't care at all. I squeezed her as close as I could. I was just so glad we'd found her.

Banana barked again as Isabel and Sadie came into sight. They took one look at her and burst into laughter. "I guess Banana chose her own costume for the parade," Sadie said. "She's going as a swamp monster!"

"I told you she has a talent for rolling in stinky things," I said. I picked some crushed egg shells out of her fur. Banana wiggled her butt, clearly feeling pleased with herself. The yellow ribbon on her collar was smeared with green sludge.

Isabel crouched beside me and hugged Banana too. "I'm sorry I called you a big meanie," she said to me.

"And I'm sorry I acted like one," I said. "Thanks for helping me find Banana anyway."

"Of course," Isabel said. "She's our favorite dog too, you know."

I grinned. "I know."

I didn't have a leash, so I picked up Banana to carry her back to the house. "Come on, smelly dog," I said. "Let's take you home."

Chapter Seventeen

Git Along, Little Doggies

When we came in the front door, Chuck was there by the stairs, swinging off the banister. "There you are!" he said. "Dad says we're leaving in twelve minutes, or the parade will start without you."

"Twelve minutes!" I cried, setting Banana down. We'd never get her cleaned up by then.

Chuck smirked. "Hey, Anna," he said. "You've got something on your shirt." I looked down at the special polka-dot top I'd chosen to wear in the parade. It was all smudged with dirt. So were my skirt and bare arms. I was almost as filthy as Banana.

"Oh no," I moaned.

Sadie grabbed my hand and pulled me up the stairs. Isabel and Banana were right behind us. "Okay, here's the plan," Sadie said. "Anna, you change your clothes and wash the dirt off your arms. Isabel and I will clean up Banana."

"But there's no time for a bath! We'll miss the parade!" I said.

Sadie shook her head. "We'll wipe her down with washcloths instead. It will have to do. Now go!"

I ran to my dresser and pulled out a new outfit, grateful that Sadie had come up with a plan.

By the time I was washed up and had changed into the clean top and leggings, Isabel and Sadie had gotten Banana mostly cleaned up too. She wasn't anywhere near as shiny and soft as before, but at least she was no longer disgusting.

"What about the costume?" I said. "Maybe she should wear it, since there's no time to brush her with olive oil, and the bow got all dirty."

"Only if you want her to," Sadie said. "She's your dog, so you can decide."

"I don't think she needs it, but it would be fun," Isabel said.

"Let's try it," I said, picking up the wings. But as I approached, Banana scampered over to Isabel. She nudged at Isabel's shin.

I laughed. "Banana thinks *you* should wear the wings," I said. Banana thumped her tail. She definitely didn't want to wear them herself. I turned back to the costume pile. "And for Sadie, the tiara?" I suggested. Banana kept wiggling. I took that as a yes. "And I'll wear the antennae headband."

"And the tulle skirt," Sadie said.

Isabel slipped on the butterfly wings. "Banana is a genius," she said. Sadie and I agreed.

"Dad's in the car!" Chuck shouted up the stairs, and a second later, we heard the horn honk. We ran down to get in the minivan, but there was one more thing I had to do before we left. I headed toward the kitchen.

"Oh yeah!" Sadie said. "We need to bring the entry form."

I grabbed the paper and a pen. "Hold on. I didn't finish filling it out."

"You can write in your address in the car," Isabel said.

"But I also need to add *this*," I said. Underneath the space for *Owner*, I added a new line that said *Best friends*, and wrote in Sadie's and Isabel's names. "There," I said.

Banana wagged her approval as we dashed out the door.

Chapter Eighteen
A Winning Idea

Thanks to Sadie and Isabel and our quick team-work, we made it to the parade on time. We checked in at the registration table, handed in our form, and lined up with Banana in the sea of other dogs. Excitement tingled through me, from my antennae to my sparkly toes.

There were cute dogs all around us—big ones, small ones, long-haired ones, short-haired ones, and everything in between. There was an orange-and-white dog with a big, fluffy tail he waved high like a flag. There was a dark brown dog with shy eyes and a sweet face who nuzzled

Isabel's hand when she patted him. He was wearing a vest that said ADOPT ME. There was a funny old dog with a plump belly and short legs, who was there with her skinny, long-legged dog cousin. The skinny one reminded me of that word of the day, "sprightly." She definitely had lots of energy.

The pair bounced right over to greet Banana. The dogs circled each other, making a tangle of their leashes.

"They're sniffing out the competition," Isabel joked as the three dogs smelled each other's butts. Sadie wrinkled her nose.

"That's how they say hello!" I explained.

Sadie straightened her tiara. "I think I'll stick with waving," she said.

The trumpeter in the marching band blasted his horn, signaling it was time for the parade to start. The band marched out ahead of us, playing a toe-tapping tune, and one by one the dogs and their owners fell into step behind them. Banana lifted her ears and walked perfectly straight as I held on to her leash, just like we'd practiced. Isabel and Sadie walked on either side of me, giggling at the tiny dog in a dinosaur costume who was marching right behind us.

We paraded through the middle of Piddleton Park, waving at Mom, Dad, and Chuck, and all the other people who'd come out to see the show. My heart thumped with gladness, in time with the beat of the drum. I couldn't think of anything better than sharing this moment with my two best friends. It was so much more fun than it would have been if Banana and I had done the parade without them.

"Look, there's the judges' booth!" Isabel said, pointing toward a platform decorated with streamers and a HAPPY HOMES ANIMAL SHELTER banner marked with paw prints.

Sadie nudged me. "Are you ready?" she said.

"For what?" I asked.

She reached into her dress pocket and pulled out Banana's squeaky rabbit toy. "For the trick," she said. "It's Banana's cutest talent."

Sadie held out the toy and I took it with my free hand. I paused for just a second before offering her Banana's leash. "Here," I said.

"Are you sure?" she asked.

"Positive," I said. I pushed it into her hand.

We took a few more steps and before I knew it, we were right there in front of the judges. My stomach was doing somersaults, but Banana didn't look nervous at all. She stared up at the toy in my hand with her eyes bright and her ears perked, looking cuter than ever.

Isabel twirled in a circle, her wings flapping. "Introducing . . . BANANA!" she yelled, spreading her arms wide.

Everyone turned to look at us. Sadie stood

up straighter and held on to Banana's leash as I tossed the yellow rabbit into the air. Banana jumped up high and caught it midtoss, then flipped it out of her mouth and caught it again. People all around us clapped and cheered. Banana trotted proudly forward, biting down on the toy to make it squeak. Sadie and Isabel and I beamed at each other. That had been perfect.

Sadie handed me back the leash.

"Did you see?" Isabel said. "Ms. Burland is one of the judges!"

"No!" Banana and I turned around to look. Sure enough, there was our teacher, sitting tall in the booth with the two other judges. I waved and Ms. Burland gave us a thumbs-up. It was kind of weird to see her outside of school, but I was so glad she'd gotten to see Banana, and that she'd witnessed our fancy trick. I hadn't realized Ms. Burland volunteered at the animal shelter. That made me like her even more.

It didn't even matter if we won a prize or not. Parading down the street with my friends by my side, I already felt like the Luckiest in Show.

Chapter Nineteen
Best of the Best

Banana carried her toy all the way to the finish line, where Mom and Dad and Chuck were waiting. Mom had a peanut butter dog treat for Banana and chocolate-chip muffins for us.

"Huzzah!" Dad cheered. He gave each of us a high five, even Banana. "That was some parade."

"Thanks!" I took a bite of my muffin and lengthened Banana's leash so she could tumble with her sprightly doggy friend from before, who'd just bounded over to us with her short-legged cousin. The dogs pounced and played as Mom chatted with the silver-haired couple

holding their leashes. Behind them, a family with three kids gathered around the sweet dog in the ADOPT ME vest. I had a feeling they'd be taking him home.

A lady in an official-looking visor walked over. "Congratulations," she said, handing Sadie, Isabel, and me each a blue ribbon.

Isabel's eyes went wide and Sadie bounced up and down. "We won?" Sadie asked.

"Everybody wins!" the lady said. "That's your prize for participating."

"Oh," Sadie said. I could tell she was trying not to look disappointed.

"How nice," Mom said. Behind her, Chuck rolled his eyes.

"So why were there even judges, then?" Sadie said as the lady walked away.

Isabel shrugged. "That did make it more fun," she pointed out. I nodded. She was right.

Isabel let Banana lick the muffin crumbs from her fingertips. "Did you notice Ms. Burland's shoes? The toes looked like ladybugs!"

"Ms. Burland's shoes could have their own parade," I said, picturing the whole colorful collection dancing down the street, toes and heels tapping.

"She's definitely Best in Shoe," Isabel said. Even Chuck laughed at that.

"I still think we should have won something," Sadie said. "Banana was a star."

I took the blue ribbon from her hands. "I hereby declare you Best Special Surprise Planner," I said, pinning the ribbon to Sadie's shirt. "That was some trick we pulled off!" I turned to Isabel. "You win Best Showmanship," I said, pinning her ribbon on too. "And I win Best Dog and Best Friends, because I have both."

Sadie and Isabel glowed. "Together we are definitely Best in Show," Sadie said. Banana barked and spun in a circle. I bent down to kiss her.

"You are most definitely the Most Bananas," I said.

Chapter Twenty
A Photo Finish

The next morning, I pinned my ribbon to my pajama top and Banana and I went down for breakfast. My parents were already there in the kitchen, reading the Sunday newspaper.

"Hey, kiddo," Dad said as he poured more coffee into his and Mom's cups. Dad turned his favorite mug so the words on it, TOP DOG, were facing toward me. "I might have to let Banana drink her coffee out of this, after that great showing in the parade yesterday," he joked.

I giggled. "Dogs don't drink coffee, Dad," I said. I poured some kibble into Banana's dish and helped myself to the Gorilla Grams. "May I please have the funnies?" I asked, sliding into a seat next to Mom. Since Chuck wasn't up yet, I'd get to read the comics section first.

"Sure," Mom said, taking it out for me. "But I think you might want to read the front page before that."

Before I could say, "No, thanks," she placed the paper in front of me, and I gasped. There, at the top of the page, was a huge photo from the dog parade. It was a picture of Sadie, Isabel, Banana, and me, right at the moment when Banana leaped up to catch her toy. Banana's ears were flying, Isabel's arms were spread wide, and all four of us had huge smiles on our faces. Under the photo was the caption *Best Teamwork*.

I couldn't believe it. Banana was famous! And

so were my friends and I. "Can we frame it?" I asked. "And get copies for Sadie and Isabel too?"

"Good idea," Mom said. I bent down to show Banana the photo. Her eyes went wide with surprise.

"Hey, Dad," I said. "Would you rather have all the riches in the world and as much coffee as you could drink, or no coffee and no mansion but two really wonderful friends?"

"Good friends," Dad said. "Definitely."

"Me too," I said. Banana thumped her tail in agreement. I smiled down at her and thought, *Lucky us.*

BEST TEAMWORK

Acknowledgments

Thank you, Kristin Ostby, grand marshal of this parade, for leading the march with such gusto (and saving me from marching in circles).

A trumpeted fanfare of thanks to designer Laurent Linn, illustrator Meg Park, and the whole fabulous team at S&S, especially Mekisha Telfer and Audrey Gibbons.

Meredith Kaffel Simonoff, I twirl my baton for you.

Sparkliest confetti thanks to the friends who help keep my balloons aloft, especially Robin, Terra, Andy, and Johanna, and to Mama, Ati, Jeremy, Erika, Anna, and Sophia, the finest bugle corps around.

First-place ribbons and chocolate-chip muffins for all the booksellers, librarians, teachers, and readers in the Page-turners' Parade.

Rooga and Jeff, you are my Best in Show.

Collect all four books in the Anna, Banana series!